Give Us A Smile,

beetle bailey®

by Mort Walker

JOVE BOOKS, NEW YORK

GIVE US A SMILE, BEETLE BAILEY

A Jove Book / published by arrangement with
King Features Syndicate, Inc.

PRINTING HISTORY
Tempo edition / May 1978
Jove edition / November 1988

ISBN: 0-515-09861-2

Jove Books are published by The Berkley Publishing Group,
200 Madison Avenue, New York, New York 10016.
The name "JOVE" and the "J" logo
are trademarks belonging to Jove Publications, Inc.

PRINTED IN THE UNITED STATES OF AMERICA

10 9 8 7 6 5 4 3 2 1

QUACK! QUACK!

WHY DID YOU DO THAT?

ANYTHING TO CONFUSE THE ENEMY